KT-562-050

A STEVEN SPIELBERG PRESENTATION
OF A DON BLUTH FILM

AN AMERICAN TAIL™

Little Lost Fievel

by **Michael Teitelbaum**
From a screenplay by **Judy Freudberg** and **Tony Geiss**
Based upon characters created by **David Kirschner**
Illustrations from the Don Bluth film

First published in the USA by Grosset and Dunlap, a division of The Putnam Publishing Group, 1986
First published in the UK by Scholastic Publications Ltd., 1987
Copyright © Universal City Studios, Inc., and U-Drive Productions, Inc., 1986

An American Tail and *An American Tail logo* are trademarks of Universal City Studios, Inc., and U-Drive
Productions, Inc.

ISBN 0 590 70762 0

Made and printed in Hong Kong

Hippo Books
Scholastic Publications Limited
London

When a little mouse named Fievel Mousekewitz was seven years old his whole life changed. Fievel and his family lived in Russia. They were a poor, but loving family who were happy as long as they were all together.

One day a terrible thing happened to the Mousekewitzes. A gang of cats destroyed their little village, and the family was forced to leave their beloved home. It was then that Papa Mousekewitz decided that the family would go to America.

The Mousekewitzes found themselves on a crowded boat travelling across the ocean, on their way to America. A storm had hit the boat, rocking it back and forth, tossing it among the waves.

"Sit down, Fievel!" exclaimed Papa Mousekewitz, as his curious son ran up a flight of stairs that led to the main deck. "Come back!"

By the time Fievel heard his father's warning, it was too late. A large wave crashed onto the deck of the ship, picked Fievel up, and washed him overboard. "Papa! Papa!" he cried, as the boat carrying his family pulled away from him. It was no use, Fievel Mousekewitz was all alone.

Fievel climbed into an empty bottle that floated by, and eventually washed up on the shores of Bedloe's Island. There he met a friendly pigeon. "Where am I?" Fievel asked.

"Why, you're in America!" answered the pigeon with pride.

"Then I must begin looking for my family at once!" stated Fievel.

The pigeon offered to help, and with Fievel on his back he soared off into the sky. He dropped Fievel off at the immigration building. "If they are on that boat, then they'll have to come through here," said the pigeon. "I've got to be going. Good-bye, and good luck."

"Thank you!" shouted Fievel, waving as the pigeon flew off and disappeared from view.

Fievel started to watch mice stream through the immigration building. He watched for a little while, but there was no sign of his family.

What Fievel did not know was that he had missed his family by only a few minutes! The Mousekewitzes had already passed through the immigration building, and had moved on to New York City. "If only we were all together," Papa Mousekewitz had said sadly, as they set out to begin their new life in America without their son.

Fievel grew very sad. Suddenly someone stopped next to him. "Warren T. Rat's my name," said the strange looking fellow. "Why are you so sad?"

"I'm looking for my family," moaned Fievel.

"Good thing you ran into me then," said Warren T. Rat. "I know exactly where they are. Come with me."

Feivel followed Warren T. Rat into New York City. His hopes were high, but they were soon shattered. Warren T. Rat had tricked Fievel! He took the young mouse to a sweatshop where many other mice were working very, very hard making clothing, for very little money. "But, what about my family?" asked Fievel.

"Forget your family, kid. Just get to work!" growled Moe, the nasty rat in charge of the sweatshop.

Fievel was very unhappy. He wanted to leave this terrible place to continue the search for his family, but he saw no way to escape.

Then Fievel made a real friend named Tony Toponi. Tony was an immigrant mouse from Italy, who was an orphan. He felt sorry for Fievel and wanted to help him find his family. Together they formed a plan to escape. They tied several suits together to form one long chain of suits. Then they tied one end to a table, threw the other end out of the window, and scampered away to freedom.

"Come on," said Tony. "Let's go and find your family." But when Tony looked up, Fievel was gone.

Fievel had spotted a big mouse in Russian clothing. He was sure it was his Papa. "Papa! Papa! It's me, Fievel!" he shouted as he ran after the mouse. Just as Fievel caught up to the large mouse, the mouse turned round. It was not Papa. Fievel sighed with disappointment. Then he realized that he had lost his friend Tony. Once again he was left all alone.

Fievel wandered the streets of New York. Every time he saw someone dressed like his Mama or Papa he would rush over to them, and every time it would turn out to be someone else.

Fievel stopped at a window and peeked in. Inside was a schoolroom. Fievel could see the happy faces of mice his own age reciting their "ABCs" while the teacher looked on, pleased with her pupils. Fievel's heart sank. He thought of happy days in school with his friends back home, "I wish we'd never left Russia," he muttered to himself, as he kept on walking.

Meanwhile, the Mousekewitz family themselves were very sad. Each day, as they walked around the streets of New York, they kept the small hope alive that they would spot Fievel. "I miss my boy so much," cried Mama and Papa too.

As for Tony, he and his friend Bridget, an Irish immigrant, searched the streets looking for his little friend. He called out Fievel's name, but his cries went unanswered.

It began to grow late, and Fievel began to get very hungry. He passed an Italian restaurant. Pressing his nose against the window pane, he looked in and saw a happy family of mice enjoying their dinner and each other's company. His stomach growled with emptiness, and his heart sank a little bit farther.

The sweet strains of violin music snapped Fievel out of his gloomy mood. "Papa!" he exclaimed. Papa Mousekewitz always played the violin back in Russia, and the music Fievel now heard coming from a nearby building sounded very familiar.

Fievel scrambled quickly up the side of the building, scampered across a clothesline, and peered into a window. He expected to see Papa playing his violin. What he saw instead was a gramophone playing a record.

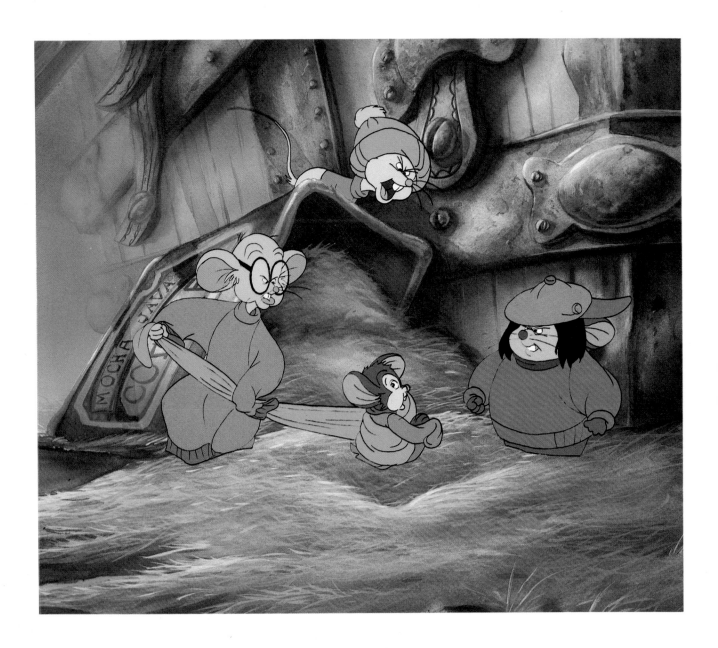

Fievel returned to the street, thinking that he would never find his family. He met a group of street mice, and settled in to spend the night with them.

"What's your story?" asked one of the homeless mice.

"I've been looking for my family," answered Fievel. "But now I'm never going to find them."

But just then, Fievel heard a violin. This time he was sure
it was not a record. "Papa!" he shouted, jumping to his feet.
"Can it really be you?"

He dashed down the street, and when he turned the
corner he saw Papa, Mama, and his sister Tanya, along with
Tony and Bridget. They had all met looking for Fievel, and now
finally the little mouse was reunited with his family.

"Oh, Papa, Mama," cried Fievel. "I missed you so much!"

"Yes, but now we are all together," said Papa. "And now we
can truly begin our new life in America."